SUKI
and the Invisible Peacock

SUKI
Silver Anniversary Edition

Suki and the Invisible Peacock
Suki and the Old Umbrella
Suki and the Magic Sand Dollar
Suki and the Wonder Star

Also by Joyce Blackburn

Sir Wilfred Grenfell: Doctor and Explorer

Theodore Roosevelt: Statesman and Naturalist

*John Adams: Farmer from Braintree;
Champion of Independence*

*Martha Berry: A Woman of Courageous Spirit
and Bold Dreams*

James Edward Oglethorpe

*George Wythe of Williamsburg: Teacher of Jefferson
and Signer of the Declaration of Independence*

The Earth Is the Lord's?

Roads to Reality

A Book of Praises

*The Bloody Summer of 1742:
A Colonial Boy's Journal*

*Phoebe's Secret Diary:
Daily Life and First Romance
of a Colonial Girl, 1742*

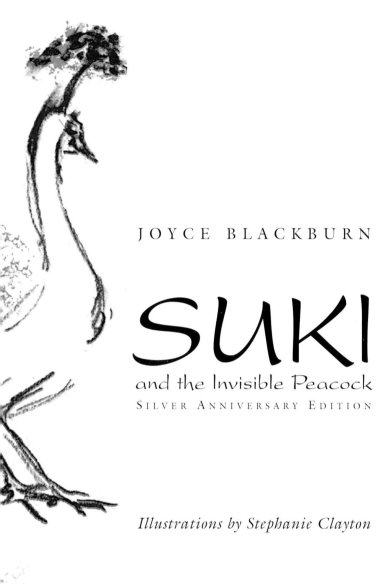

JOYCE BLACKBURN

SUKI
and the Invisible Peacock
SILVER ANNIVERSARY EDITION

Illustrations by Stephanie Clayton

PROVIDENCE HOUSE PUBLISHERS
Franklin, Tennessee

First edition 1965. Second edition 1996
Printed in the United States of America

00   99   98   97   96   5   4   3   2   1

Library of Congress Cataloging-in-Publication Data

Blackburn, Joyce.
    Suki and the invisible peacock / Joyce Blackburn ; illustrations by Stephanie Clayton. — 2nd ed.
        p.   cm.
    Summary: Suki's life is changed when the invisible peacock living in her backyard becomes her best friend.
    ISBN 1-881576-69-8
    [1. Friendship—Fiction. 2. Imaginary playmates—Fiction.
3. Peacocks—Fiction. 4. Japanese Americans—Fiction.]
I. Clayton, Stephanie, ill. II. Title.
PZ7.B53223Su   1996
[Fic]—dc20   96–14852
                                                                      CIP
                                                                       AC

Cover design by Schwalb Creative Communications Inc.

PROVIDENCE HOUSE PUBLISHERS
238 Seaboard Lane • Franklin, Tennessee 37067 • 800-321-5692

For
Nancy Fuji
Mark and Tom
Cindy
David
Amy
and
Katie

The Way Things
Were Before

Suki looked at herself in the mirror, the one on the medicine cabinet. She had to stretch on her toes and brace her arms stiffly to be able to see anything. The mirror was for big people.

All she wanted to see were her sound, even teeth. After brushing them her mouth felt tingly and cool. It even looked cool.

"Suki, hurry up!" a sharp voice called, "Are you going to stay in there all day?"

The doorknob rattled.

Suki hated shrill voices. She hated having to hurry early in the morning.

It was always the same . . . every school day. Her older sisters nagged and threatened until she opened the bathroom door. There they stood, both of them, waiting to take their turns and looking very superior.

As she dressed, the voices chased her up and down the hall, "Suki, hurry up! Your muffin is getting cold!"

By the time she sat down at the breakfast table *they* were shoving back their chairs and gathering up their books. She knew the next cry would be, "Suki, hurry up! If you aren't ready we're going on without you."

As if she cared. As if she wanted to walk to school with them . . . and their friends. All of them would crowd together and talk big secrets and pose and giggle. They acted as though she weren't there.

That was why she poked along half a block behind her older sisters. Alone, you can take your time. You notice important things . . . spider webs and wiggly cracks in the sidewalk and clouds with faces.

Of course, it would be nice to have a best friend to notice important things with you. . . .

1

Did you ever visit the zoo?

    Suki did.

Did you ever watch the peacocks at the zoo?

    Suki did.

Did you ever hear the peacocks shout?

    Help!

        Help!

            Help!

    Suki did.

That was how Suki decided a peacock was beside her as she stood at the corner waiting for the traffic light to turn green. She could not see a peacock. But she was sure she could hear "Help! Help! Help!"

Everyone was staring at Suki. A cab slowed down,
and the jolly driver called, "You'll make it by
yourself, little girl. Don't be scared."

He probably thought *she* was shouting "Help!
Help! Help!"

Only Suki knew there was a peacock standing
next to her on the curb, and it sounded exactly like
the one she had heard at the zoo. Even though she
could not see him she felt sorry for him and said,
"What is the matter? Why are you crying *help?*"

"Because I cannot cross this wide busy street
alone," said an oldish, raspish voice.

The traffic light turned green. In that instant
Suki swooped up the Invisible Peacock in her arms
and hurried across the street. As she carefully set him
down she thought:

I must be dreaming . . . I feel so
foolish . . . I do hope no one is watching.

"No one is," said the Peacock as though Suki had spoken her thoughts aloud.

"How did you know what I was thinking?" Suki asked the Invisible Peacock.

"Well, I do not want you to think I am bragging," he answered, "but I am very, very wise."

He said this so naturally and so humbly that Suki imagined him to be the very wisest and the very kindest creature in all the world.

From this moment she would trust him with all her thoughts and dreams and secret wishes.

They walked side by side . . . Suki's feet scarcely touching the ground.

At last Suki had found a best friend.

2

Six hours later, Suki hurried through the huge double doors of the Louisa May Alcott School into the spring sunlight.

Six hours had never lasted so long!

The clock had never been so poky!

Suki had tried her best to listen to the teacher. She had tried her best to study in the library. But the truth was she had not heard one word. She had not read one word.

The Invisible Peacock was the *only* thing Suki could think about.

Would he be waiting now? He had promised to meet her by the new maple tree . . . the one her class had planted. Was he there? Or had she *imagined*

their walk to school that morning? Maybe she had
not really heard him cry

       Help!

          Help!

             Help!

after all. Mother was always saying, "Suki, your
imagination is running away with you again!"

And her two older sisters would say, "Suki,
you're just making that up!"

Once when her Daddy had overheard them, he
said slowly and softly, "Imagination is the beginning
of faith. I want you to have faith when you grow up,
Suki." She could not guess what all that meant, but
the way Daddy looked at her told her imagination
was a *good* thing to have.

"It can play tricks on you, though," she said
right out loud.

"Not this time."

It was the Invisible Peacock. Suki was sure she
heard him say, "Not this time."

He was not waiting by the new maple tree. He
was already beside her going down the school steps.
He had kept his promise like a best friend always
does.

"Didn't you think I would come?" asked the
Invisible Peacock.

"Yes and no," Suki replied smiling. "Mostly yes."

At that moment, the
big boy they all called Butch
shoved Suki from behind. Then as
he leaped down the steps he yelled:

*Slant Eyes is talking to
herself again!*

Dozens of girls and boys were
coming out the school doors now,
shouting and teasing, chasing past
like jets. But Suki was watching
Butch disappear. She made a face
and muttered:

I hate him . . . I hate him.

That was how she forgot
all the lovely things she had
thought up to tell her best
friend. Instead, she began
telling him about Butch.
She was all wound up.
She talked faster and
faster and faster.

Butch was a pest. He simply would not leave her alone . . . he tripped her at recess . . . he stole a bouquet of daisies she had brought for Miss Kelly . . . and tore them up, petal by petal . . . he stepped on her clean sneakers . . . he wrote his name in bright green ink all over her English workbook . . . *and* every time he got caught doing something he knew he shouldn't do . . . he would blame the other kids . . . but worse than that he had to tell on everybody. Butch was a mean old tattletale!

The Invisible Peacock thought Suki would never have finished the list if she hadn't run out of breath.

"Hmm. Tattling *is* pretty serious," he said, "but have you never told on your sisters?"

Suki stopped perfectly still, and her face turned red all over.

"Just once," she squeaked, "and I'm still sorry. You *would* have to know about that!"

"Oh, it doesn't change anything," the Invisible Peacock chuckled, "I love you just the same. I even love Butch."

"*You—love—Butch?*"

Suki would have to think that over . . . carefully. Her best friend even loved Butch! Nothing more was said as they walked the long block to the very corner where they had met the first time. Could that have been only this morning?

3

This time there was no waiting for the traffic light. It winked green, and the two friends crossed the wide busy street quickly.

"I must go home now. My mother and daddy will be watching for me," Suki told the Invisible Peacock. "What will you do?"

"I'd better get back to the zoo," he sighed.

"You don't like it there, do you?" Suki asked.

"Let's say I like the jungle better."

"Jungle! What jungle?" One of Suki's favorite books was about a boy who lived and hunted in a jungle. "What jungle?"

"The very densest, greenest jungle in all of India," replied the Invisible Peacock.

"India! But that's so far, far away! You must be homesick."

"Some days are harder than others," the Peacock said simply. "India is a very large place, and my jungle was always warm and full of flowers. The yard at the zoo is a little crowded, and it gets pretty chilly when the wind blows off the lake."

Suki couldn't bear for her best friend to be lonely in the strange city zoo.

"You must come home with me." It was a command. "I live on this street a block north.

Downstairs is my daddy's gift shop.

Upstairs is our home.

In the backyard is a *beautiful* Paradise tree.

Until I met you, it was my best friend. One branch has grown as high as my bedroom window. A month from now the leaves will be so thick I can lean out of my window and touch them. You can stay there. It will be your very own place and I will be close by. We will be together."

"Thank you. I will be honored to come."

The Invisible Peacock spoke as though he had just been invited to the grandest palace by his favorite princess.

As they arrived at her father's gift shop, the little girl stooped down and said, "My name is Suki. Say it."

"Suki," the Peacock whispered.

"And I will call you Best Friend. Don't forget."

Her hand turned the cool, smooth knob, and the familiar door opened. A little bell tinkled and Suki and the Invisible Peacock stepped inside.

4

The Gosho Gift Shop was one narrow room softly lit.

The Invisible Peacock squinted and sniffed. Was that a faint scent of sandalwood in the air? He liked that. It reminded him of India.

The big bird looked slowly up and down, around and around, raising and lowering his long neck. Every inch of space on the shelves was filled. Earth-brown pottery teapots . . . porcelain vases and bowls . . . bronze figurines . . . lacquered trays and nests of boxes . . . baskets of wrapping papers . . . green and gold, pink and purple. Long and short and middle-sized backscratchers, carved from ivory, hung on tasseled, scarlet cords.

He knew each one like an old friend. They had come all the way from the Far East packed in plain, excelsior-stuffed boxes. Now, here they were, for sale in the Gosho Gift Shop. But to the Peacock they were like jewels full of the mystery and color of his homeland.

From the rear of the shop a small man walked toward Suki and the Invisible Peacock. His face was as round as a narcissus bulb. Only his eyes smiled. And he hugged Suki with pleasure.

"Daddy, I've brought along my best friend," she whispered. "He is an invisible peacock I met on the way to school."

Her father did not so much as blink. "A peacock you met on the way to school? Interesting. Where did he come from, Suki?"

"Oh, from a jungle in India . . . a jungle full of flowers. But lately he has been staying at the zoo, and, Daddy, you know how crowded and bare it is there. May we let him stay in our Paradise tree? *Please*? At least for the summer?"

"Certainly," Daddy said at once. "Tell your friend we will be honored to have him."

"Did you hear that, Best Friend?" Suki clapped her hands. "Oh, you are the best, best daddy in all the world!" Suki cried, almost smothering him in a

storm of pats and kisses. They laughed so loudly that Mother came to see what was going on.

"Have you two *wrinkled sillies* gone out of your minds?" she called above the merry shrieks.

Her voice was sharp, but her black eyes danced. She liked to have Suki and Daddy play their games.

She liked to hear them laugh. It brought the quiet little shop to life, and it made her heart all warm and happy.

"Mother, guess what? My best friend has come home with me to stay. Daddy says he can!"

"What best friend is this, Suki . . . another stray dog or cat? You know we haven't room."

"No, Mother.
            He isn't a dog.
                  He isn't a cat.
                        He's an invisible peacock,
and he's going to live in our Paradise tree."

"An invisible peacock?" Mother winked at Daddy. "Suki, your imagination is running away with you again!" she said as she hurried from the room.

Daddy looked almost as disappointed as Suki did. But he kept a smile in his voice as he said, "Some things are real even if we can't see them. I can't see my Best Friend either."

"Who, Daddy? Who is your best friend?"

"God. God is everyone's Best Friend, Suki."

Suki thought a minute. "What's God really like?"

"Love, Suki. He *is* Love. Even when we are bad, He loves us. When we feel no one cares about us, He cares. When we're alone, we can talk to Him, the way you talk to the Invisible Peacock, and He is right here with us . . . all the time."

Daddy looked at the silver watch on his wrist, then at the pretty blue clock on the wall. "Say, my watch is slow again. I didn't know it was almost time to close the shop."

Suki looked at the clock on the wall, too. Its face was flat and white, framed in the pretty blue. The short black hand pointed to five. The long hand was still an inch away from twelve.

Now Daddy would roll up the scalloped yellow awning. Her sisters would come home from their swimming lessons. The front door would be bolted. The safe locked up.

The Gosho Gift Shop would wait silently through the long night.

The Invisible Peacock followed Suki into the back hall which was still bright with afternoon sun. Mother was going up the stairs.

"Come inside soon, dear," she said to Suki, "we'll have an early supper. Daddy has to go to the Park-West neighborhood meeting."

"All right, Mother," Suki called running out the door.

The yard was as long and narrow as the shop. A gravel path wound among low evergreens and flowering bushes to the tall back fence. And close to the house was the Paradise tree. The Invisible Peacock spotted it at once.

"This is it, Best Friend. What do you think of it?"

"I think it is the loveliest tree I have ever seen, Suki, and that's saying something."

He could see that the sapling tree had grown crooked and low to the earth. Now the old trunk curved gradually skyward to where the branches reached. They were heavy with buds. Spring rains and sun would push out the spear-shaped leaves, and a patch of cool, cool shade would spread over the ground below. Yes, the Peacock could see it all. He could feel the shade.

"You wouldn't guess it, Suki, but this tree and I have something in common. It lost its leaves late last summer, didn't it?"

"Yes, and I got so tired of raking."

"Well, I lost the feathers in my train at about the same time."

"You did?" Suki gasped, "Did that hurt very much?"

"Ho! Ho! Not at all. We peacocks always lose our longest feathers then, the ones that extend beyond our tails, but new ones replace them."

"The way the tree gets brand new leaves?"

"Exactly."

"Do tell me more about yourself, Best Friend."

Suki perched herself on a large flat rock under the Paradise tree, and the Invisible Peacock hopped up beside her. "How long will it take to grow your fan again? Is that what you call it, a fan? How long will the feathers be? And what color?"

"Hold on a minute." Best Friend chuckled, raising a foot in protest, "If everything turns out all right my train will be six feet long by next Christmas."

"Six feet long. Why, that's seventy-two inches!"

"Exactly. You notice I call it my *train*. Some peacocks call it a *halo*. Scientists call it a *nautch*. You call it a *fan*. No matter what it is called it is forever giving me trouble."

The Peacock shook his feathers as though this talk made him uncomfortable, and he began to pace up and down in front of Suki. She couldn't see his eyes. He turned his head away. But she did hear a sadness in his voice when he said slowly, "I haven't told anyone this before, but I can tell you . . . I wish my fan would never grow back."

"What a terrible thing to say, Best Friend. I have never seen anything so beautiful as a peacock with his feathers spread."

"That's just the point," moaned the bird, "day after day people came to visit our yard at the zoo. And whether they were three years old or eighty they all said the very same thing. They would walk up close to my fence and say:

Come on! Spread your tail!

Every single one of them said it:

Come on! Spread your tail!

"So I always did . . . to please them. Now, it's tricky to balance a huge fan of feathers like that when you spread it out as far as it will go, and you have to lift your feet high and gallantly to keep from falling on your face. They would say:

Isn't that gorgeous!

"They would say that all right, but then I would hear:

What a vain bird he must be! Look at him strut!
Look at him strut! Thinks he's something!
Proud as a peacock! Ha!

"They said it every time, Suki. Every time. And they laughed. It made me want to disappear. I prayed the earth would open up and swallow me. That's why I became invisible."

Suki put out her hand to touch Best Friend. She stroked the fine feathers on his neck and whispered, "I'm so sorry . . . so sorry. Those people were cruel. What you've told me just makes me love you more, and I know you are not beautiful only when you spread your tail. You're beautiful on the inside all the time and you're not proud. You're humble. Truly humble. I know! Best Friend, you are going to stay with me, and that tree," she pointed, "is your very own home, and you won't have to show anyone your fan if you don't want to . . . not ever!"

31

The lovely moment was shattered by the squeak of the screen door. Mother stood there, tying on her apron.

"Suki, your sisters have come. Get ready for supper now."

"Good-bye for a little while," Suki said to the Peacock. "I'll bring something for you to eat. Watch for me. That's my window . . . the one closest to the top of the tree. It won't be long."

Best Friend saw Suki disappear inside the house. Then he pecked curiously at the gravel and swallowed a few grains of sand.

"For the first time in weeks I believe I'm hungry," he mused. "It will soon be dark. I wonder if I can make it up to that limb outside her window."

He started walking up the curved trunk of the Paradise tree. The first limb was close to the second. He flew straight up. Then to the next . . . and the next.

"Thirty feet, at least," exclaimed the Invisible Peacock looking down to the ground. "My, I haven't been this high since I was a pea-biddy in the jungle!" He cautiously edged out onto the swaying limb until he was opposite Suki's window. And with perfect balance, he settled himself to wait.

5

With her fork Suki drew flowers and fancy doodles on the soft white tablecloth, then erased them with one magic stroke.

She had not listened to the conversation at the supper table, but she knew her sisters had done most of the talking. You would think no one ever took swimming lessons before.

The words had swirled around her, and the faces above the steaming plates bobbed and blurred while she dreamed of a tropical jungle far away, swarming with color . . . birds . . . insects . . . flowers . . . snakes . . . furry animals . . . scaly animals. . . .

"Suki, you haven't touched your fruit."

Mother's voice startled her so she dropped her fork, and it clattered to the floor.

"Eat your raspberries, Suki, so that I can clear the table."

"Raspberries are too pretty to eat, Mother. I don't think I care for any."

"Nonsense, Suki. You haven't eaten enough to keep a canary alive."

Mother began stacking plates and bowls for Suki's sisters to take to the kitchen. Daddy folded his napkin and looked straight at Suki. She was sure he was going to say the same thing Mother had said, but he fooled her.

"Did you know that peacocks like raspberries, Suki?"

Mother was making such a racket she didn't hear what Daddy said, but of course Suki did. Then an idea popped into Suki's head just like that.

"Mother, may I take my bowl of raspberries to my room?"

"Yes, dear, just so you eat something."

Suki tried not to hurry as she folded her napkin the way everyone else had and excused herself from the table. She pranced out of the room holding the bowl of berries high over her head and smiled triumphantly at Daddy. He smiled back.

The Invisible Peacock waited patiently. From his perch on the limb outside Suki's window he could see inside even though it was getting dark.

Suddenly a light went on, and there she was, coming toward him. She set the bowl on the wide sill and raised the window as high as it would go.

"Did you think I was never coming, Best Friend? Supper took forever. But look at what I've brought you. They're fresh ones too." Suki shook some of the berries out of the bowl into her hand. "You must be starved!"

The peacock had not had a bite to eat all day, but he was too polite to gobble up the handful of berries the way he wanted to. Instead he suggested:

"I want you to share them with me, Suki. They will taste better if you do."

"All right. Let's make up a game. I'll have one . . . then you. The last berry makes the winner!" As the bowl emptied, they ate faster and faster until the very last raspberry was swallowed. "Best Friend is the winner!" Suki laughed, "Three cheers for Best Friend! "

Both of them felt the hush the dark was bringing, and it quickly quieted them. "This has been the best day," Suki whispered, "I don't want it to end."

"I know," said the Invisible Peacock, "it is always that way with happy days. We never want them to end. But they seem to fly. It's the sad ones that drag by."

"You *are* wise, Best Friend."

"I have lived a long time, Suki. The years have taught me. You are a little girl, but I am thirty years old."

"Why, you're as old as my daddy. I never dreamed peacocks got to be as old as parents!"

"Oh, yes, peacocks often live to be *forty*. But if I should live to be that old, I know there will not be a lovelier day than this one. I shall always remember the way you understood when I told you how I felt at the zoo, and the way you shared your Paradise tree and the beautiful raspberries."

"That's the way it is with best friends," Suki said softly. "Good night."

"Good night, Suki."

6

The next day was Saturday.

From a great distance Suki heard the rumble of trucks and the tinkle of a bell. The sounds whirled around in her dream in grand confusion, then gradually separated and came closer until she could place them. The trucks were in the alley. The bell was downstairs in her father's shop. She didn't open her eyes though. Not yet. She never liked to wake up suddenly.

What was *that* funny sound? It was closer than the others. Suki opened her eyes sleepily. Her room was full of morning sun. Then she remembered. Best Friend! That funny sound must be Best Friend pecking on her window. She was out of bed in an instant and raised the window with a bang.

"Oh, Best Friend, why didn't you wake me sooner?" she cried. "This is Saturday, and I don't have to go to school . . . we'll have the day all to ourselves."

"And what a perfect day it is," exclaimed the Invisible Peacock. "A perfect spring day."

Suki thought his voice sounded almost young; not nearly as raspish as yesterday. *Why, he sounded happy. That's what it was . . . the touch of sadness was missing.*

"Won't you have to help your mother at home today, Suki?" asked Best Friend.

"Yes . . . some. On Saturdays I clean my room and go on errands, but that won't take long," she told him. "This is a busy day in the shop so it's better if I'm not around. Anyway, there's something I especially like to do on Saturdays."

Best Friend was immediately curious. "Such as?"

"I don't think I'll tell you," Suki teased. "That way it will be a surprise. Don't you love surprises? I do. If I were you, I wouldn't want to know. I'd rather be surprised."

Best Friend laughed. "All right, you surprise me. When will that be?"

"I'll hurry with my room and have breakfast. By the way, what do you like to eat besides raspberries?" Suki giggled. "Didn't we have fun last night, playing eat-the-berries?"

"Yes, Suki, that was a new game to me. Well, now . . . let me think about what I'd like to eat." The Invisible Peacock closed his eyes and concentrated.

"Best Friend, what peculiar eyes you have! They don't close down like mine do, they close up. Your eyelids turn up from the bottom!" Suki reached out and pulled the big bird's head close to her and examined his eyes.

"It's a good thing my neck is so elastic," he complained good-naturedly, "or I might lose my balance and slip off this limb." He pretended to steady himself.

"So, you think my eyelids are different from yours. They are. They work just the opposite way from yours. Watch . . . I'll shut them very slowly. As I close my eyes my eyelids come up. When I open my eyes, my eyelids go down."

Suki was spellbound. "Do it again," she ordered. "Open. Close. Open. Close. Best Friend, you know what? I always wake up. You wake *down*!" She was delighted with this discovery and kissed him impulsively on the top of his head.

"Quick. Tell me what you like to eat."

"Well, greens . . . any kind of greens, but my favorite is kale, *kurly* kale."

"Oh, I just love *kurly* kale," Suki interrupted.

"Shelled corn makes a good solid meal," continued the peacock, "and next to raspberries I like worms for dessert."

"Worms! Ugh!" Suki held her stomach.

"Oh, you won't have to bother with the worms," he continued. "I'll find my own. But let's not waste anymore time. You do your work, and I'll explore the yard." With that the peacock dropped down to the limb below, then gracefully glided to the ground.

"You'll like what we're going to do today," Suki called. Leaning much too far out of the window, she waved, then ducked inside.

It was almost noon when they met again and started down the street together. So far, the Invisible Peacock knew where he was. This was the way they had gone to the school.

But a half block further on Suki turned into a narrow passage between two high apartment buildings. At the end of the passage stood four huge garbage cans, and once they had squeezed past them they came out into an alley. Now, some city alleys are deserted and lonely, but this alley was bustling with activity. Along the other side of it a whole block of old, worn out buildings was being torn down.

Piles of rubble . . . bricks . . . stone . . . glass . . . shingles . . . discarded doors and rusty bathtubs . . . piles of rubble too high to see over, lined the alley.

They had been made by a monster machine that swung an iron ball from a crane. The ball must have weighed tons and tons. And every time it thudded against one of those old walls the bricks would crumble apart and fall to the ground . . .

C-R-A-S-H !

The noise was deafening. The clouds of dust and plaster were suffocating. But all the children in the neighborhood watched spellbound, Saturday after Saturday. During school days a guard kept them away, but he was off-duty on weekends. It was a dangerous place, but after all, that was what made it so exciting.

"This is going to be the school playground when they get finished," Suki shouted to Best Friend above the noise. They had found a safe place for

themselves between two piles of bricks that gave them a good view.

Suki turned an old crate on its side and propped herself upon it ready for a long "watch." The Invisible Peacock leaned against it too. He didn't like the noise, but he wasn't going to spoil Suki's fun.

Finally, during a lull, he asked, "Does your father know you come over here?"

"Oh, yes," Suki said, "he brought me the first time. He brought my sisters too. Of course, I have promised him to be very, very careful not to get close to the buildings. Goodness! If one of those walls toppled over on you they might *never* find you!" Her body shivered with horror—the kind she enjoyed.

"Look, there's Butch and that mean gang of boys he's always playing with."

The Invisible Peacock had seen them before Suki did. They were climbing the piles of rubble and throwing rocks at the windows in the walls still standing. One of the workmen in a steel helmet yelled at them, "You know you're not supposed to be out here. Scram! All of you! Beat it!"

Showing off as usual, Butch leaped down from the pile of bricks and began chasing another boy. They veered and headed straight for Suki sitting on the edge of the crate. Before she knew what was happening the first boy jumped right over her, just missing her head.

She knew Butch was going to try it too! Suki crouched down holding Best Friend tight against her as Butch sailed over them and landed

K-E-R-P-L-U-N-K

on his bottom . . . all 110 pounds of him.

"Butch!" Suki screamed, running to him, "did you hurt yourself, Butch?"

"Don't touch me!" the big boy growled. "Tried to make me break my neck, didn't you, Slant Eyes? Well, it didn't work, see!" He scrambled to his feet.

"The next time you get in my way, I'm going to take care of you, Slant Eyes. Understand?" Butch shook his fist and acted as if he were going to hit her.

46

Suki was scared, but she managed to say:

"I didn't make you fall, Butch. I didn't do anything to you. Honest! And my Best Friend and I are sorry if you hurt yourself."

"What best friend?" jeered Butch.

"My Best Friend, the Peacock."

"I don't see any peacock."

"Maybe you don't," said Suki, "but I do, and he's staying in my Paradise tree."

"Crazy! Loony! That's what you are, Slant Eyes! All girls are loony!"

And with that Butch tore off to find his buddy. They would cause more trouble around the next corner. You could be sure of that.

7

"Come on, Best Friend, let's go home. I don't want to watch anymore."

Suki shoved the crate away and kicked at a piece of old brick. The Invisible Peacock could tell she had hurt her toe on the brick, but he said nothing, and followed her back through the narrow passage between the apartment buildings.

When they reached the sunny street, he rearranged his feathers, and said cheerfully, "It is still a beautiful afternoon, Suki."

She didn't answer. It was as though she had forgotten he was there.

"I heard Butch call you Slant Eyes," he said, looking at her lovingly. "When you laughed at my eyes this morning I didn't get angry, did I?"

"No, of course not, Best Friend, but I wasn't making fun of your eyes! I laughed because they were so different."

"Exactly. And that's what Butch thinks about yours. Tell me, Suki, do *you* like your eyes?"

Suki thought for a moment. "Yes, I like my eyes. They're different looking because I'm Japanese-American. *Nisei*, Daddy says. But that's all right, isn't it?"

"Is it all right for a peacock to have eyelids that close up instead of down like yours do? Is it all right for an Indian peacock to live in a tree in Chicago, Illinois, U.S.A.?"

"Oh, yes!" exclaimed Suki.

"The point is, peacocks are peacocks," the big bird said.

"And people are people. Is that what you mean, Best Friend?"

49

"Exactly. That's the most important thing to know, and Butch hasn't found it out yet. He's not the only one, I'm sorry to say. Lots of people act like differences are more important than being friends."

"I wonder if that's why they make up names like Slant Eyes?" Suki asked thoughtfully.

"Exactly," said the Peacock, using his favorite word again.

The anger and fear inside Suki melted, and she wished she could think of a way to help Butch understand about people the way the Invisible Peacock had helped her.

With a great sigh of relief, she said, "You're right, Best Friend, it is still a beautiful afternoon. Let's go back and watch some more."

Suki had just placed the crate again where she wanted it, and Best Friend had just cozied down beside her, when the monster ball and the monster steam shovel and the monster tractors suddenly went silent. It was as though someone pushed a button and turned them all off at once. The workmen took off their helmets and goggles and gloves. It was 12:30 P.M. Saturday, and time to quit.

When the workmen were gone there was nothing more to see until Monday. Everyone who had been watching left too. Everyone except Suki and Best Friend. They didn't budge.

"Poor old houses," Suki mused, "think of all the people they have kept warm. Now they have no windows . . . no doors . . . no chimneys . . . no roofs . . . just some walls. Don't they make you feel sad, Best Friend?"

"Yes, Suki, they do, but I like to think about the playground for all the school children that's going to be here one day, then I'm not sad anymore."

"Look!" Suki said, "somebody painted something on that old wall. That wasn't there last Saturday. Let's go see what it is, Best Friend."

They got up and walked toward the wall. Big letters had been painted on it. "DANGER," Suki read, "FALLING BRICK. KEEP AWAY."

Most of the wall had already toppled into a great gaping hole beside it that had once been a basement.

"We mustn't go any closer," Suki warned, "It says DANGER."

"Listen!" whispered the Invisible Peacock, "I thought I heard something . . . down in that hole!"

They stood perfectly still and listened.

"There! I hear it too.

Sounds like a groan!" Suki said, and inched closer.

They heard it again . . . louder this time. "Someone *is* groaning," Suki said in alarm. "I wish I dared get close enough to see."

"I can," said the Invisible Peacock, "I can crane my long neck like a snake, right over the edge."

Carefully they looked down into the deep, dark trench the steam shovel had dug along the wall. Giant wooden beams had fallen across one end, and on top of them a section of the old wall. And it must have just happened, because the dust was still thick enough to make it hard to see. They could hear the groans plainly.

"Someone is buried under the bricks," Suki cried. "I can't see him, but he's groaning. He's hurt!"

Suddenly bricks began rolling in all directions, and a boy's head appeared. "It's Butch, Best Friend! It's Butch! Those old bricks tumbled in on him. We'll have to get help!"

Butch must have heard her because he tried to call, "Suki, is that you?" His voice was hoarse and scared. "Suki, get me out of here!"

Suki and Best Friend could see Butch clearly now. He was working his shoulders and arms free. Perspiration poured down his dirty face from the effort, and there was blood on his T-shirt.

"I'll run home and get my daddy!" Suki called.

"No, don't leave me, Suki," Butch begged, "just yell. Someone will hear you. Yell, Suki! Hurry!"

Suki was so weak with fear she knew her voice would never attract anyone's attention. She tried to call but she might as well have been whispering.

Then she remembered how peacocks shout, and she pretended she was a peacock. "Help! Help! Help!" It was a hair-raising, piercing cry.

"Help! Help! Help!"

To Suki her voice sounded magnified a thousand times. It echoed above the piles of rubble and brought people running from their houses. "Help! Help! Help!"

Suki didn't pause. "Help! Help! Help!"

A blue and white squad car squealed around the corner into the alley. It pulled up close to Suki, and a policeman jumped out.

"Stand back!" he shouted at the people crowding around. "What's going on?" he asked Suki.

"Butch—Butch is down there!" she pointed. "The wall fell on him. He's under the bricks!"

8

Daddy held the door of the automatic elevator open for Suki and the Invisible Peacock.

She had not stopped talking all the way to the hospital, but once they entered the lobby she was too busy looking at everything to say much. The big door clicked shut.

Daddy pressed a button marked 4, and they began floating upward.

"We've never visited anyone in the hospital before, have we, Daddy?"

"No, Suki. But hospitals are wonderful places for sick people. This is the very best place for Butch to be until the doctors and nurses find out how seriously he was injured."

Daddy had listened to every word Suki told him when she and Best Friend reached home after the accident. Of course, Suki's sisters said the same old thing, "Suki, you're just making that up." But Mother seemed proud of her for helping to rescue Butch. And she suggested that Daddy take Suki to the hospital to see him.

"Here we are," Daddy said as the elevator stopped and the door opened.

To the left was a high counter, and behind it sat a nurse in her crisp uniform writing a report.

"Pardon me," Daddy said, "we would like to see a boy named Butch. They told me at the main desk in the lobby that you would know the room number."

The nurse checked a list. "That must be the boy they brought up from X-ray a while ago. He's in 411." She gestured with her pen.

"Thank you," Daddy said politely.

The hospital corridor was painted a soft green, and the floor was spotlessly clean. Suki had expected it to be unfriendly, but it wasn't. She could hear people talking and laughing in the rooms they passed, and someone was watching a circus on television.

But circuses didn't interest Suki now. Suddenly there was a cold, hollow place down inside her that made her want to turn around and go back home. Even her legs felt wobbly. She hoped Daddy wouldn't notice. They were passing 407. Room 411 was only four doors away.

Suki thought: *What if Butch calls me Slant Eyes when I go in to see him? What if Butch won't be friends?*

Because she had been in such a hurry to get to the hospital, that thought hadn't entered her head until this moment. It jolted her the way a volleyball did once at school when it hit her in the stomach; it knocked the breath out of her, and it made her sick.

"Daddy . . . I'm scared!"

"Of what, Suki?"

"Of seeing Butch, I guess."

"Oh, I doubt that he was hurt that bad, Suki. You said he was conscious, and the bricks didn't fall on his head."

"It isn't that, Daddy." Her voice sounded faint. "What if Butch still hates me?"

The door of 411 was open, but they stopped outside and Daddy took Suki's hand and squeezed it . . . hard.

"The important thing is, how do *you* feel about *him*?"

Suki didn't say anything. She was hearing Best Friend say (that long ago day when they first met), "I even love Butch . . . I even love Butch . . . I even love Butch. . . ."

When they walked into the room Butch was propped up in the high hospital bed, his face as white as the pillows. Daddy gave Suki a little nudge, then stepped back into the hall to wait. She walked across the room and stood beside the bed.

"Hello, Butch. Are you all right?" she asked shyly.

"Yeah, I guess so, Suki." It was the first time he had ever smiled at her. She had never seen Butch's face so clean. She hadn't even noticed his freckles before.

"Will you have to stay in the hospital long?"

"The doctor didn't say. I probably have some bad bruises . . . and a cracked rib. That's all."

Suki said what she had heard grown-ups say, "It could have been *worse*, Butch."

"Yeah. I heard the doctor tell my uncle that I was the luckiest kid on the whole North Side."

"Your uncle?" Suki asked surprised. "Doesn't your mother know about the accident?"

"My mother is dead, Suki." Butch tried to turn over on his side, but it hurt too much. "I live with my uncle and spend vacations in Montana with Dad."

"Will your daddy come to see you in the hospital?"

Butch looked out the window at a pigeon sailing in wide circles against the sky before he said, "No, he won't come. That would cost too much . . . on top of the hospital bill."

Suki was puzzled. "But he likes you, doesn't he?"

Butch tossed his head in the same old cocky way, "Sure, he likes me . . . so what? If he doesn't . . . so what?"

"I like you, Butch." For the first time she knew she did, whether Butch liked her or not.

"You like me . . . after the way I've treated you, Suki?"

She wished Butch would stop looking at the pigeon and look at her. "We can forget that," she said, "as though it never happened." And then he did look at her.

"Boy! I never heard anybody yell the way you did, Suki." There was admiration in his voice now. "It's a wonder the whole police force didn't show up!"

"I didn't think the police or the ambulance would ever get there, did you, Butch?"

"It seemed like a week to me. How could you yell so long?"

"Oh, I couldn't have ever done it, Butch, without Best Friend to help me."

"Best Friend? What are you talking about? . . . you were all by yourself." Butch frowned. "Is Best Friend a joke or something?"

"No, he isn't a joke at all," Suki said. "He's an invisible peacock, and he lives in our Paradise tree, and he's the wisest and the kindest creature in all the world, and he's my best friend. I want you to meet him, Butch."

"Yeah, if he's your best friend, I sure want to."

Suki leaned down and said softly, "Best Friend, you told me that you loved me . . . and Butch too, didn't you?"

"Does he really talk to you?" Butch asked in amazement.

"Oh, yes, Butch. My daddy says some things are real even if we can't see them. You *are* real, aren't you, Best Friend? And your love is real . . . as real as sunlight . . . and you love me all the time, no matter where I am, no matter what I am doing . . . whether I'm good or whether I'm bad."

Butch's face lit up. "Is that the way love is, Suki?"

"Exactly!" said Suki looking straight into Butch's blue eyes.

"Well, that's the way . . . you make me feel . . . Suki," Butch stammered. "*You* make me feel . . . all full of sunlight!"

"I do, Butch . . . I do?"

This was the most exciting afternoon of her whole life! She wanted it to go on and on, but she had already stayed longer than she was supposed to stay, so she said, "Best Friend and I must go now. But we'll come back."

"Is that a promise?"

"That's a promise, Butch."

She waved good-bye from the doorway and skipped up to Daddy waiting in the corridor.

As they entered the elevator she said, "Wait, Daddy . . . Best Friend's tail isn't in!"

Daddy smiled to himself and thought: *What an imagination that child has. She's just like me.*

Aloud he said, "When we get home, Suki, I have a treat for you and Best Friend."

"Oh, tell us now, Daddy . . . what is it?"

"A basket of *kurly* kale!" Daddy said.

And they all laughed.

Joyce Blackburn has written fifteen published books since leaving a professional career in Chicago radio. Her recording of *Suki and the Invisible Peacock* led to a contract for her first book of the same title. Subsequent prize-winning titles for young readers have made Blackburn well-known among librarians and teachers. She has also gained recognition in the field of popular historical biography and enjoys an enthusiastic adult following. Blackburn, a resident of St. Simons Island, Georgia, received the 1996 Governor's Award in the humanities from the Georgia Humanities Council. Her works are in the Special Collections of the Woodruff Library at Emory University, Atlanta, Georgia.